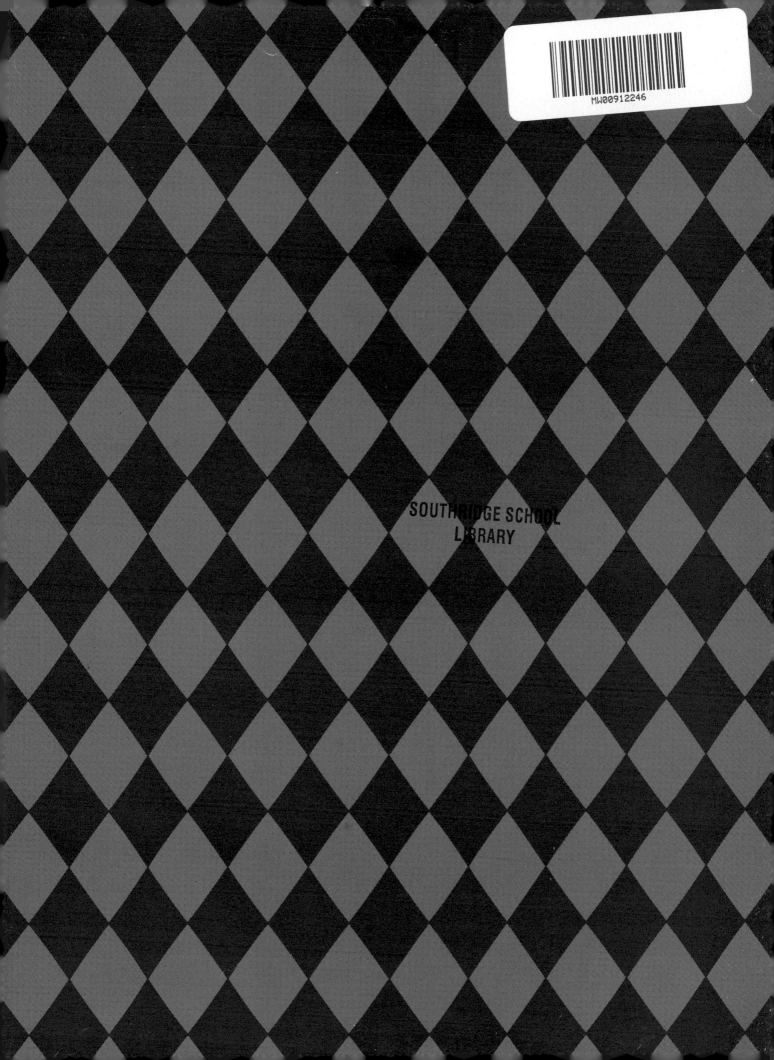

THE
PARROT

An Italian Folktale Retold and Illustrated by

LASZLO & RAFFAELLA GAL

A GROUNDWOOD BOOK
Toronto Vancouver Buffalo

Groundwood Books / Douglas & McIntyre
585 Bloor Street West,
Toronto, Ontario M6G 1K5

Distributed in the United States by
Publishers Group West
4065 Hollis Street, Emeryville CA 94608

The publisher gratefully acknowledges the
assistance of the Canada Council and the
Ontario Arts Council.

Library of Congress data is available.

Canadian Cataloguing in Publication Data

Gal, Laszlo
The parrot : an Italian folktale

"A Groundwood book".
ISBN 0-88899-287-4

I. Tales - Italy. 2. Parrots - Folklore.
I. Gal, Raffaella, 1969-   . II. Title.

PS8563.A39P37 1997 j398.2'0945'0452871
C97-930049-5 PZ8.1.G35Pa 1997

Special thanks to Luigi Speca of Malabar Ltd.
for his generous assistance. — LG
The illustrations are done in colored pencils,
oil and egg tempera on board.
Printed and bound in China by
Everbest Printing Co. Ltd.

For Cecilia Mattolini with affection
For Nonna Mary con amore

ONCE upon a time in
an ancient kingdom
there lived a merchant and
his beautiful daughter.

On the top of the mountain that loomed over the village stood the castle of the king. He was a wicked old man who was wildly in love with the maiden. He often peered at the merchant's house through a spy glass, hoping to catch a glimpse of her.

But a young prince from a neighboring kingdom also loved her. The prince, suspecting that the king had evil plans for the maiden, moved to the village so he could watch over her.

One day the prince learned that the merchant had to leave his daughter behind while he went abroad to sell his goods. He was very worried. What would the king do while the merchant was gone?

The prince thought and thought. Finally he had a plan.

He went deep into the woods to visit a famous sorceress.

"Can you teach me to become a parrot whenever I want?" he asked.

"Certainly," she said. And she did.

The prince turned himself into a parrot and flew to the merchant's house. When the girl saw him perched on a pear tree outside the window, she opened it. Immediately the parrot flew in and began to amuse the maiden with his talk.

The more stories he told, the more she wanted to hear. Finally the parrot said, "If you promise not to interrupt, I will tell you the most marvelous tale in the world. But you must not let anyone or anything stop my story, or I will have to leave, and you will never know the ending."

At that very moment there was loud knocking at the door. The wicked king had sent his soldiers to fetch the maiden. But she told them that she was too busy to see anyone, no matter how important. She settled down and begged the parrot to begin.

"Very well," said the parrot. "But *no* interruptions."

Once upon a time there was a king who had a daughter who was as beautiful as you–well, almost as beautiful. Because she had no brothers or sisters, the king gave orders to his best artists and artisans to create a doll that looked exactly like her.

After a few months, a marvelous creation was presented to the king. It was a doll that indeed looked just like his daughter. The princess was so happy with her magnificent gift that she took it with her everywhere.

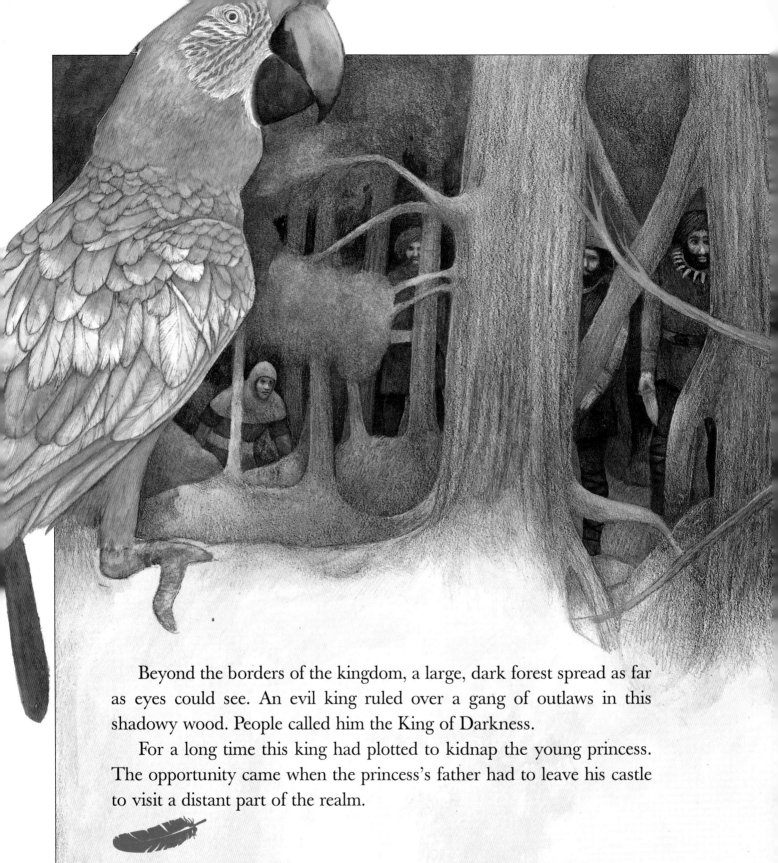

Beyond the borders of the kingdom, a large, dark forest spread as far as eyes could see. An evil king ruled over a gang of outlaws in this shadowy wood. People called him the King of Darkness.

For a long time this king had plotted to kidnap the young princess. The opportunity came when the princess's father had to leave his castle to visit a distant part of the realm.

Knock, knock, knock.

"Go on. Go on," said the princess to the parrot. "I told you not to interrupt!" she told the king's soldiers. "The story is just getting interesting."

The King of Darkness ordered two of his men to kidnap the princess, who was alone in the palace. When night fell, they scaled the wall of the tower to her apartments.

The princess was getting ready to go to bed. She placed her doll on a chair and went to the other side of the apartment to prepare her bath. The two ruffians broke into the dimly lit bedroom. They seized the doll, and in an instant they were climbing down the rope.

"Is that all? Tell me what happened next," begged the princess.

The parrot went on.

The bandits rode all night. But when dawn came they saw to their dismay that the doll was not real. Fearing the wrath of the king, they threw it down by the side of the road and fled.

A prince riding by later in the day saw the beautiful creature and carried it back to his palace.

Knock! Knock! Knock!

Louder came the pounding on the door. The maiden shooed the soldiers away again.

"Please, please go on," she begged the parrot. "Don't stop now when it's getting so exciting."

"Very well," said the parrot, "but any more interruptions and I'll have to stop."

When the princess's father returned, he realized that the kidnappers had really been after his daughter, and he promised never to leave her alone again.

The next time he went for a trip, he took his daughter with him. The trip was long and arduous, so at one point they stopped to rest. The forest floor was covered with the most beautiful flowers. The princess couldn't resist the fragrances and colors, so while her father was dozing, she picked a few, then some more, slowly moving away from the carriage.

When the princess finally returned to the carriage, she found it overturned. Her father and his servants had all disappeared.

Disconsolate, she set out to search for him. She wandered in the forest for days. She collected berries, nuts and wild mushrooms to eat.

One night, as she was about to fall asleep under a rock ledge, she heard voices. A short distance away she saw a fire burning. She groped her way toward the light until she was close enough to make out the faces of five terrifying ...

Bang! Bang! Bang! on the door.

"For goodness' sake," begged the maiden. "Tell them to go away and please go on."

Well, what she saw were five terrifying witches cooking something horrible over an open fire. Snakes and frogs flew into the pot as the witches croaked like huge ravens.

"A spell, a spell. To kill a prince."

"Where will we find him, Sisters?" asked one of the witches.

"We found him in his bedroom pining with love for a doll," answered another. "We have placed him in a dungeon hidden right below his very own castle. Only we knew there was a passage under his bed." And they cackled.

The princess slowly crept away. Then she rode all night. By the time the sun was rising over the horizon, the forest was far behind her. By noon she was at the gate of a big city. Black flags were flying from the windows of every house.

"The prince has disappeared. We fear he is dead," the baker's wife told her when she stopped to buy bread.

When the princess heard this, she went straight to the palace.

"Let me in," she said to the guards. "I have very important information about the prince."

The queen and her guards rushed to find the prince. There he was where the maiden had said. They rescued him, but he didn't seem to care. He simply sat staring at the doll without moving. Nothing the queen could say or do made any difference.

The despairing queen looked more closely at the doll, and she noticed how much it resembled the beautiful stranger who had told them where to find the prince.

"Run and see if that maiden is still in the castle," she commanded.

The guards found her just as she was setting off to search for her father again. When they brought her to the royal family, the prince suddenly awoke from his spell.

"You, you are the one I love," he called out. "Will you marry me?"

"But my father is lost. I must find him," said the princess sadly.

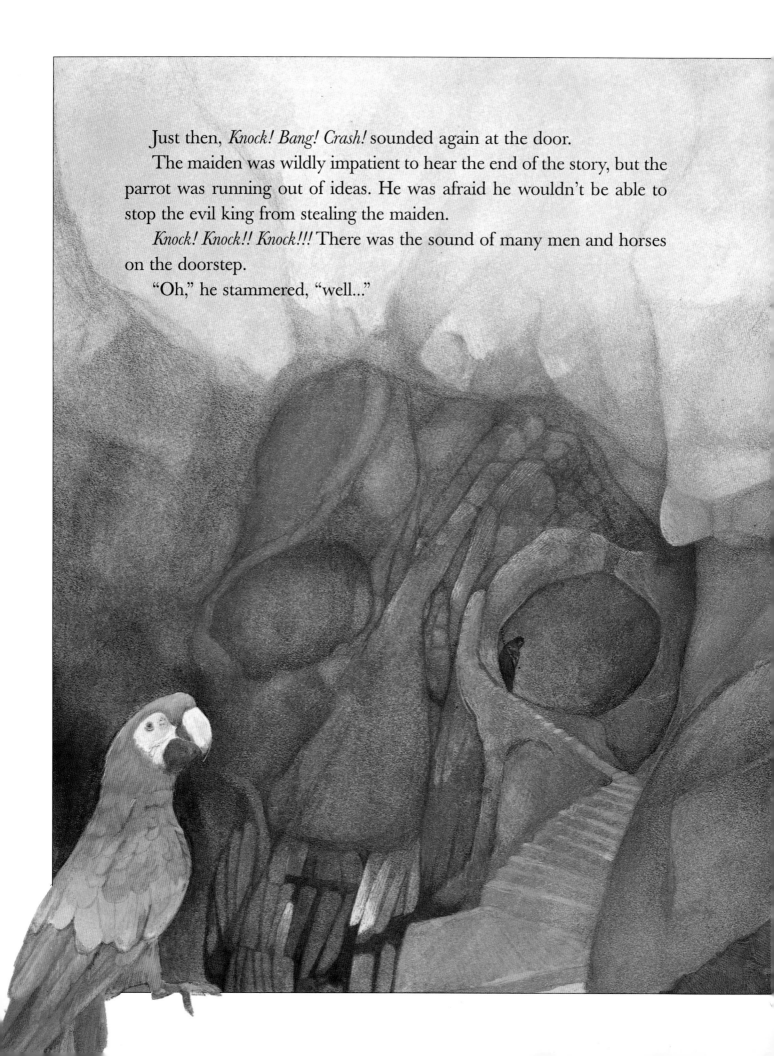

Just then, *Knock! Bang! Crash!* sounded again at the door.

The maiden was wildly impatient to hear the end of the story, but the parrot was running out of ideas. He was afraid he wouldn't be able to stop the evil king from stealing the maiden.

Knock! Knock!! Knock!!! There was the sound of many men and horses on the doorstep.

"Oh," he stammered, "well..."

The queen and the prince agreed to go with the princess to help her find her father, and they did. Then they got married and lived happily ever after, and then...

Suddenly they heard a shout at the door.

"It's your father. Why won't you let me in?"

The maiden rushed to the door and there was the merchant, back from his trip.

"Oh, Father," she exclaimed. "The most wonderful parrot has been telling me the most magical story. It went on for days and days. And because he couldn't tell me unless no one interrupted, I never answered the door the whole time you were away. Come and see what a magical bird he is."

But in the other room stood a handsome young man. The parrot was gone.

"Please forgive me," he said to the maiden. "The wicked king had planned to steal you away." He explained that he was a prince and had become a parrot in order to keep her from the grasp of the horrible king.

"Furthermore," he said, "I hope you will marry me."

"Of course I forgive you," said the maiden, laughing. "How could I say no to such a wonderful storyteller who is a prince as well."

And that is the end of that story, and the other one, too.

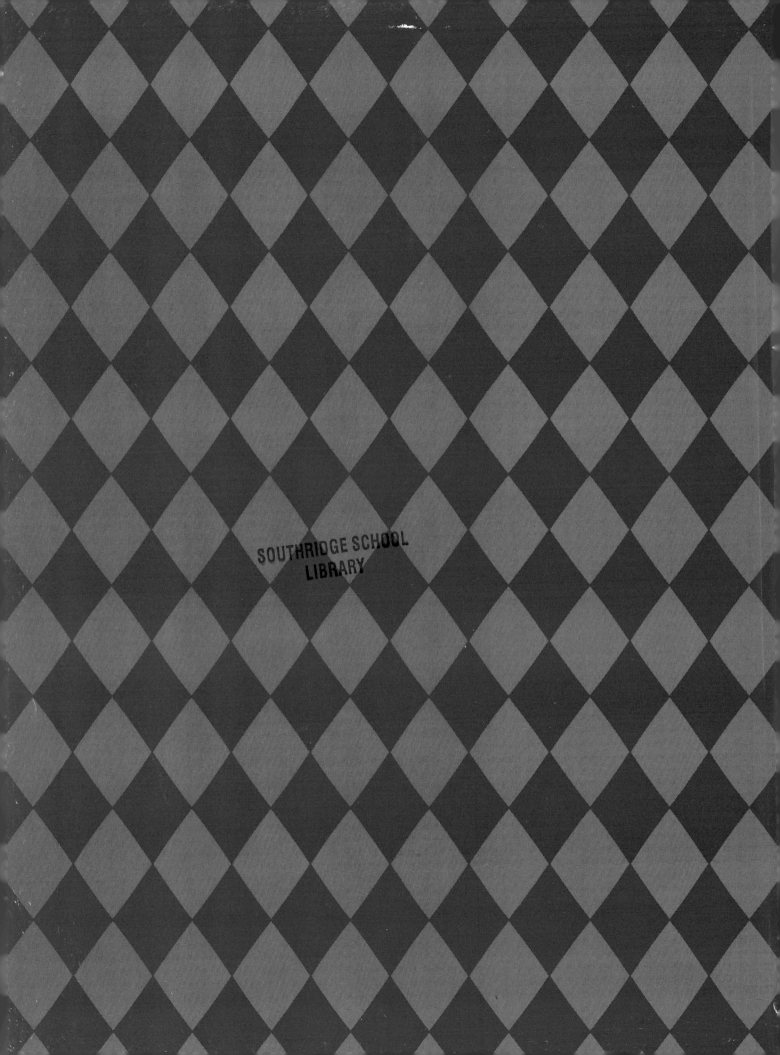